I do hope you enjoy reading *Tracy Beaker's Thumping Heart*. It's so great to remember that every time a copy of this book is sold, Comic Relief gets £2. I know just how much all children care about Comic Relief. I've seen the red noses, I've seen the scarlet hair, I've seen the funny costumes! Now you can feel you're also contributing by reading this new story about Tracy Beaker. I think it's the funniest Tracy story yet!

Tracy gets in a state on 14th February because it looks as if she isn't going to get any Valentine's cards, and her worst ever enemy Justine starts teasing her unbearably. But then little Peter declares his love for Tracy and gives her an amazing Valentine's present. This is just the start of the story. If you're a fan of Barney and Basil Brush just wait till you read about Tracy taking part in Swap Shop on television!

I'm sure you'll be watching the incredible night of TV on Friday 13th March celebrating Red Nose Day. There'll be hilarious fun and games with all your favourite celebrities – and you'll also see very moving films showing how Comic Relief helps so many people in the UK and Africa to make positive changes to their lives – people just like Tracy Beaker!

Tracy is the kind of child who has been on the receiving end of care. It's great for her to think that now she's helping others. It makes her heart go thump!

Jacqueline Wilson

Jacqueline Wilson

Tracy Beaker's Thumping Heart

Illustrated by Nick Sharratt

CORGI YEARLING

TRACY BEAKER'S THUMPING HEART
A CORGI YEARLING BOOK 978 0 440 86881 1

Published in Great Britain by Corgi Yearling,
an imprint of Random House Children's Books
A Random House Group Company

This edition published 2009

1 3 5 7 9 10 8 6 4 2

The Random House Group Limited supports the Forest Stewardship
Council (FSC), the leading international forest certification organization.
All our titles that are printed on Greenpeace-approved FSC-certified
paper carry the FSC logo. Our paper procurement policy
can be found at www.rbooks.co.uk/environment.

Set in 11.5/15.15pt New Century Schoolbook

Corgi Yearling Books are published by Random House Children's Books,
61–63 Uxbridge Road, London W5 5SA

www.kidsatrandomhouse.co.uk
www.rbooks.co.uk

Addresses for companies within The Random House Group Limited
can be found at: www.randomhouse.co.uk/offices.htm

THE RANDOM HOUSE GROUP Limited Reg. No. 954009

A CIP catalogue record for this book is available from the British Library.

Printed and bound in the UK by
CPI Bookmarque, Croydon, CR0 4TD

*To Dr Sion Gibby
Dr Arvind Vasudevas
Dr John Foran
and all the staff at
St Anthony's Hospital and
the Royal Brompton Hospital
who looked after my own
thumping heart.*

Tracy Beaker's Thumping Heart

It all started on St Valentine's Day. I'd never bothered about February 14th before. I don't go in for all that lovey-dovey slop. I certainly don't go a bundle on those sentimental satin hearts and huggy teddies and fat pink Cupid babies with wings. I'm Tracy Beaker, OK? Enough said.

The Dumping Ground

I live in a Dumping Ground. It's actually a Children's Home for looked-after kids. Ha. You only end up here if you're *not* looked after. It isn't a home at all. It's definitely a dump.

I'm only there on a temporary basis of course. My mum's coming for me soon, just you wait and see.

I know she misses me every bit as much as I miss her. It's just that she's otherwise engaged, holed up in Hollywood, making movies. She really is. Justine-Know-Nothing-Littlewood says I'm making it all up but you don't want to take any notice of *her*.

I just have to flash my special photo of my mum and it's perfectly obvious she's a film star. She's got lovely blonde wavy hair and big blue eyes and shiny pink lips. She's the prettiest woman I've ever seen in my life. Even Justine-Argy-Bargy-Littlewood doesn't dispute that.

'So how come she's got such an ugly little squirt for a daughter?' Justine said, jabbing at the photo, poking the baby Tracy right in the tummy. I'm in my mum's arms, cuddling up to her. I look cute as a button, all smiles, with tiny tufts on the top of my head. I'm not quite as cute nowadays. I generally glare rather than grin and my curls have exploded all over so that I

prod

resemble a fuzzy floor mop. However, I am still *much* better looking than Justine-Bulgy-Eyed-Bullfrog-Littlewood. I might not be a Raving Beauty but I have Character. People say this all the time. I once had a social worker who was forever calling me a Right Little Character.

Elaine the Pain

I'm not sure how my current social worker Elaine the Pain would refer to me. I would possibly have to Delete some Expletives. I have an amazing vocabulary and often use long words. Expletives are *rude* words. (I often use them too!)

I won't need a social worker when my mum puts in an appearance, obviously. I expect this will be VERY SOON, the moment she's finished her mega movie commitments. Those Hollywood moguls are certainly keeping her busy as she hasn't written to me for *ages*.

I've got Mike and Jenny, who work at the Dumping Ground, on red

NO, SORRY, TRACY

alert for any phone calls from my mum. I often ask if she's phoned. Every day. Sometimes two or three times. They always sigh and say, 'No, sorry, Tracy' in this exasperated way. Exasperated is a posh word.

It means people getting fed up with me. Folk are frequently exasperated when they deal with me.

It's not *my* fault. If only they wouldn't be so mean and give me my own mobile then I could make my own phone calls, no problem. A mobile is a bare necessity of modern life, for goodness' sake. I think it's outrageous that none of us kids in the Dumping Ground are allowed one until we're officially teenage, and even then it's a bog-standard pay-as-you-go embarrassment. Even Adele is limited to this type of manky mobile, and she's the oldest and coolest girl in the Dumping Ground. She's going to get her own flat soon. She's forever making plans for how she's going to furnish it and what she's going to do there.

'It's going to be Party Time every night of the week!' she says.

I hope she invites me to her parties. Adele is my favourite at the Dumping Ground. We hang out together lots. OK, she gets a bit Exasperated – with a capital E – when I experiment with her make-up and try walking in her amazing high heels.

4

She has been known to say, 'Jolly well clear off, Tracy Blooming Beaker' – or expletive words to that effect.

She's only kidding. She totally appreciates my company. In fact she frequently begs me to be her best friend. I might capitulate. (*Very* posh word for give in.) I very very rarely capitulate. I am one tough cookie who knows her own mind.

I *used* to be best friends with Louise. She's the prettiest kid here, with big blue eyes and long fair curls. She's *almost* as pretty as my mum. She looks as sweet as sugar but she's actually as sharp as knives. We used to have such fun together until Justine-Poach-My-Pal-Littlewood came along and stole her away from me.

Of course I could always get Louise back again as my best friend, easy peasy. But she's lost her chance. I don't *want* her now.

Adele is much more fun. Lots of people think so too. This was *abundantly* obvious on Saturday morning, Valentine's Day . . .

We were all sitting having our breakfast at the long table in the kitchen. The little kids were all strapped into their highchairs at one end, waving their soggy rusks and spooning up their mashed banana.

Maxy was kept up that end too. He's big enough to sit on a bench with us but you need to keep *way*

clear of him when he tucks into his cornflakes and slurps his orange juice. He doesn't just *spill*. He's such a greedy little beggar he gollops it all down too quickly, chokes, and then spurts it all out like a fountain – *not* a pretty sight.

The rest of us kids with passable table manners cluster together. I always used to sit beside Louise but now Justine-Jabbing-Elbows-Littlewood does her best to make me unwelcome. I generally sit next to Adele – and weedy Peter nudges up to my other side more often than not.

I haven't mentioned Peter up till now, though he actually plays an important part in this story. This is surprising because if you saw a photo of all of us kids in the Dumping Ground you'd find him the least significant. He's this weird little geeky kid with big eyes like Bambi and arms and legs as spindly as spaghetti.

He's always clutching a soggy lacy hankie in his little paw. It used to belong to his nan who looked after him until she died and little Pete got dumped alongside us. He hangs on to it like it's his cuddle blanket. It's soggy because he's frequently in tears. He's much too old for all his namby-pamby snuffles. He might only look about six but he's my age. *Exactly* my age. He has the cheek to have the same birthday as me so we have to share a birthday cake between us. We might share our star sign but we have NOTHING in common.

I never cry. I didn't even cry when Louise went off with Justine and they stole my totally private diary and wrote ludicrous lies all over it. I didn't so much as whimper when my mum forgot to send me a present last birthday. Correction: of course she sent me a present. Loads of them. A karaoke kit for definite. And maybe my own mobile, and a little laptop and an iPod and a genuine cowboy hat and new football boots, all sorts of stuff, but they somehow got lost in the post, stolen before I could lay my hands on my parcels. But I *still* didn't cry. I might have the odd attack of hayfever which everyone knows makes your eyes stream – but I never cry.

'I know you don't ever cry, Tracy,' says Peter. 'You are *soooo* brave.'

He isn't taking the micky. He idiolizes me. This is somewhat irritating. He trots round after me and hangs on my every word, no matter what. I don't *want* him acting like my little shadow. I frequently tell him to shove off. But then his little white face crumples up and he has to mop his big eyes with his Nanny rag. This is an infuriating ploy. It makes you feel mean and then you have to be sweet to him to stop him blabbing. I'll offer him a bite of my Mars bar or I'll teach him a new naughty word or if I'm *really* feeling kind I'll tickle him under his scrawny little arms. He'll nibble at the Mars and gasp at the rude word and squeal when he's tickled and tell me that I'm the best kid in the Dumping Ground. In our town, in our county, in our country, in our world, in our own ultra-extensive universe.

I just nod and go, 'Yeah yeah yeah' because I know this already. I'm Tracy Beaker, right?

So Peter was sitting next to me at breakfast on the fourteenth. He nudged up so close he was practically sitting in my lap.

'Give us a bit of elbow room, Peter,' I said, giving him a shove.

'Sorry, Tracy,' he said, but he wriggled even closer so that his mouth was right next to my ear. 'I want to ask you something,' he said, his whisper tickling terribly inside my ear.

'What?' I said loudly, rubbing my ear.

8

'Sh! It's a secret,' said Peter.

I sighed. Peter was forever telling me secrets and they weren't very exciting. He'd confide enormously embarrassing stuff, like he sometimes wet the bed at night, as if he imagined this wasn't obvious to everyone, seeing as he wandered round the Home half the night trailing damp sheets like a waterlogged ghost.

'Tracy, it's the fourteenth of February today,' Peter whispered.

'That's not a secret,' I said.

'It's Valentine's Day,' Peter persisted.

'That's not a secret *either*,' I said, exasperated.

'Tracy, will you be my Valentine sweetheart?' Peter whispered.

'What? Oh yuck, Pete, I don't believe in all that sentimental slush,' I said.

'*I* do,' said Peter. 'Oh, Tracy, please say you will.'

He blinked at me with his big Bambi eyes. Justine-Big-Nose-Littlewood was peering in our direction, looking inquisitive.

'OK, but shut up about it now, right?' I hissed.

'So that's a yes?' said Peter, kicking his legs jubilantly under the table. He just happened quite by wondrous chance to kick Justine-Daddy-Long-Legs-Littlewood right in the shins!

'Ouch!' Justine shrieked.

9

'Well *done*, Peter,' I said. I gave him such a congratulatory clap on the back he nearly shot across the table top. Maxy stopped slurping cornflakes and shrieked with delight. He choked, with predictable results.

'Simmer down, kids,' said Jenny. 'This is worse than feeding time at the zoo.'

'Yeah, yeah, me a wild animal,' said Maxy, scratching himself vigorously and snatching a plate of mashed banana from one of the babies, who started howling.

'Behave, you lot!' said Mike, wielding his big wooden spoon, pretending to rap all our knuckles.

There was another rap at the front door, an important official rat-a-tat-tat. I felt a familiar clutch at my chest. I always wondered if it could possibly be my mum come calling for me at long last. All the noise of the room faded and I just heard the thump thump thump of my heart. Then Jenny came back into the kitchen with a huge pile of post in her arms.

'It was the postie,' she said. 'Hey guys, Valentine's cards!'

The babies went on spooning their banana, Maxy elaborated on his animal

10

imitation, but the rest of us sat upright, twitching. I suddenly *got* it. It was a competition. Who was going to get the most Valentine's cards???

Jenny was sorting through them all, giggling, especially when she found a card addressed to herself. Mike had a card as well, a big funny one that played a silly tune when he opened it up.

I stared at the rest of the cards in Jenny's hands. She doled them out. One for Justine-Absolutely-Ugly-Littlewood!!! Who on *earth* would send a Valentine's card to her? She seemed thrilled with it too, reading the dumb verse over and over and stroking the glittering silver heart on the front.

'Who's it *from*, Justine?' Louise asked. 'I didn't know you had a boyfriend! What's his *name*? Look, he's signed it!'

'I'm not telling. It's a secret,' said Justine-Smug-Git-Littlewood, clapping her card to her chest.

'You haven't got a boyfriend, not unless he's blind and stupid,' I said fiercely. 'I bet you sent that card to yourself!'

'No, I didn't, Sour-Grapes-Nobody-Loves-You-Beaker,' said Justine-Smug-Bug-Littlewood.

'Take no notice, Tracy,' Peter whispered right in my ear. 'She's talking rubbish. *I* love you. I'll make you a special Valentine's card.'

11

I couldn't concentrate on Peter and his tickly whisper and his offer of a crayoned card. I reached right over the table and snatched Justine's card. I only saw it for a second before she snatched it back, acting outraged, but it was enough time to read the message and the signature. It wasn't from a boyfriend at all. The card said *To dear Justine, Happy Valentine's Day, Love from Dad*.

I felt as if I'd been stabbed in the stomach. It was much much better than a card from a stupid boyfriend. I didn't even *have* a dad. Not that I cared. I had a mum and she was all that mattered to me. Had *she* sent me a Valentine's card?

I waited while Jenny went on dealing them all out. Louise got one. Louise got another. Louise got *three*! They were all from boys at school. They were all nuts about her. She kept giggling, pink in the face, *sooo* pleased.

'Hey, Louise has got *three* valentines, look!' crowed Justine-Brag-A-Lot-Littlewood. 'Louise has got more Valentines than anyone else. So that proves she's the most popular girl here.'

'Not absolutely accurate,' said Adele, as Jenny gave her a *handful* of cards, one, two, three, four, *five* Valentines. The last was a huge one with a big red satin heart and a badge saying *Happy Valentine, Love you Lots, Babe.* Adele chuckled and pinned it on her top.

'Adele's got *five* Valentines, way more than anyone else in the whole Dumping Ground,' I said. 'So *she's* the most popular girl, right?'

'Adele doesn't properly count. She's not really a girl, she's nearly grown up, and she's got heaps of boyfriends anyway,' said Justine-Pedant-Littlewood. 'Louise got the most Valentines of all us kids. And I've got the prettiest Valentine because of all the silver glitter and the lovely verse. What have you got, Tracy Beaker? Absolute *zilch.'*

'That's all *you* know, Justine-Rubbish-Littlewood,' I said.

Jenny still had a few cards left. Maybe maybe maybe one was for *me.* If Justine's dad had sent her a card maybe my mum *might* just have decided to send me a Valentine. It would be a cool way for her to keep in touch. Maybe she'd write a special message: *To my darling little Tracy, Happy Valentine's Day, See you Very Soon, Lots of love, Mum.*

13

Jenny kept handing out the cards. She held up the last one, giggling, because it was another one addressed to *her*.

'Don't look so desperate, Tracy Beaker. Look, she's nearly in tears. Boo-hoo baby. Fancy getting in such a stupid state. No one would ever dream of sending *you* a Valentine,' said Justine Asking-For-A-Punch-Littlewood.

'That's just where you're wrong,' I said. I spoke slightly indistinctly.

'Absolutely one hundred percent wrong,' said Peter. 'I happen to know Tracy will be getting an enormous and very special card as soon as possible.'

'We don't count scribbly home-made efforts from little weeds,' said Justine-Crushing-Littlewood.

'She's not just getting a card, she's getting a Valentine's *present*!' Peter declared. 'She's getting it right this minute. Just you wait till you see what it is.'

He jumped off the bench and ran out of the room. Justine and Louise tittered together, while Mike went, 'Aaaah!' and Jenny went, 'Sweet!'

'I bet that's what he's going to give her – a sweet,' said Justine-Scoffing-Littlewood. 'He'll have probably sucked it first!'

Peter came charging back, carrying *something* in a tremendously sellotaped brown paper bag.

He thrust it at me triumphantly. Oh dear, oh dear, oh dear. What on earth would it be? A marble? A ten pence piece? A pebble with a message scratched in biro?

I knew just how much Justine would jeer.

'I think I'll open my parcel in private,' I said, simply trying to save Peter's feelings.

'No, no, open it *now*,' said Peter. 'You wait and see, Justine. Tracy's got a *fabulous* Valentine's present.'

'So you're giving her a Valentine's present, are you, little Petey-Wetey-Wet-The-Bed. Ah, how touching!' said Justine-Viper-Tongue-Littlewood.

Peter's white face flushed raspberry red.

'I *don't* wet the bed, Justine. And anyway, even if I did, Jenny says it's nothing at all to be ashamed of,' said Peter.

'Absolutely spot on, Peter,' said Jenny, her nose still inside her Valentine's cards. 'Come on, Tracy, open your present. We're all dying to see what it is.'

I could see there was absolutely no way I could sneak off and open Peter's wretched parcel in private. I decided to brazen it out. If Justine dared sneer I'd pick up Maxy, shoogle him violently up and down and then aim him in her direction.

I struggled with my bitten nails to prise back the sellotape. It looked as if I might need bolt-cutters. I improvised, biting my way in. I peeled back layers of crumpled tissues – and stared at Peter's Valentine's present.

'What is it, then? Let us see!' said Justine-Long-Nosed-Littlewood.

I silently held it up. It was a beautiful gold locket in the shape of a heart. Real gold. The heart was huge, almost as big as my fist. A gold heart like that must be worth hundreds and hundreds of pounds! Everyone gasped.

'Where on earth did you get *that*, Peter? You didn't nick it, did you?' said Louise.

'Don't be ridiculous, Louise,' said Jenny. She looked astounded too. 'Where *did* you get the locket from, Peter?' she asked.

'I've kept it hidden in a sock ever since I came here. It was my nan's,' said Peter. He said it proudly but his eyes filled with tears. He nearly always cried when he talked about his nan. 'She used to wear it on Sundays. It had a chain to match but I'm afraid it got broken. But the locket's still fine. Look, Tracy, you just press this little catch, see.'

He demonstrated with his small finger and the locket opened. There was a photo of an infant inside, a pale baby with little downy curls, big Bambi eyes, sticking out ears and a very skinny neck.

'That's me,' Peter said unnecessarily. He edged up to me again, whispering so the others wouldn't hear. 'Nan used to say I was her little sweetheart. Now I'm 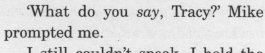 your Valentine sweetheart, aren't I, Tracy?'

I didn't know what to say. I remembered the time Mike and Jenny took all us kids to a theme park and I went on the rollercoaster. My stomach felt exactly the same now. I was touched that weedy little Peter liked me enough to give me his nan's incredibly valuable locket – but all that sentimental sweetheart stuff made me want to throw up.

'What do you *say*, Tracy?' Mike prompted me.

I still couldn't speak. I held the gold locket tight in my hand and stared hard at the table top, praying that I wasn't about to succumb to an inconvenient bout of hayfever.

Jenny put her arm round Peter.

'It's such a sweet romantic gesture, Peter, but are you really sure you want to give your nan's very special heart to Tracy?'

'Of course he's sure!' I said indignantly.

'Maybe you could give Tracy the heart just for today?' Jenny persisted.

'What kind of a rum deal is that?' I said. 'Presents are meant to be *permanent*.'

'I want to give Tracy the heart for ever and ever,' said Peter fervently.

Justine-Has-To-Mock-Littlewood made silly whistling noises, rolling her eyes. Louise and the other kids copied her – but Adele smiled.

'Aah, you're such a little gent, Pete,' she said. 'You're a very lucky girl, Tracy.'

I nodded, clutching my gold heart.

'Now you'll have to find a very special place to keep your heart, Tracy,' said Jenny. 'It must be *very* valuable. I think I'd better pop it in the safe for the moment.'

'No way! I'm wearing it!' I said.

'For goodness' sake, Tracy, you're the girl who's always losing everything,' said Jenny. 'This week it was your pen, last week your swimming kit – and didn't we have to fork out for an entire new school bag for you last month? Of course I can't let you wear a real gold locket. Anyway, you haven't got a chain.'

'I'll *make* a special chain. Oh, Jenny, please, it means so much to me. No one's ever given me such a special incredibly expensive present – apart from my mum, of course,' I said, laying it on thick.

'Go on, Jenny, let her wear her locket!' said Mike.

'All right. You can wear it at the weekends, Tracy, so long as you look after it ultra-carefully. I haven't got the heart to argue with you any more. *Heart*, get it!'

I tittered obligingly and sauntered off to manufacture my chain. Peter skipped along beside me, beaming so brightly his lips nearly met at the back of his head.

'Do you really really really like your Valentine's locket, Tracy?' he burbled.

'Yes, I do. I'm going to wear it all the time, even at school. I'll get round Jenny somehow. I can't wait to show it off. It's so big! It must be worth a fortune!'

'Well, to be absolutely truthful it isn't really worth a fortune, Tracy. It isn't actually *gold* gold,' said Peter, looking very worried.

'What are you on about? Of *course* it's gold,' I said, holding the locket up.

'It's just gold-*coloured*, Tracy. My granddad won it for my nan at a fairground. You have to keep polishing it like crazy or it goes a sort of green colour – but I've made it lovely and shiny now. It *looks* like real gold. You don't mind that it isn't *actually* gold, do you, Tracy?'

I minded terribly. I'd never owned any real jewellery before. None of the kids in the Dumping Ground had *proper* jewellery. Adele had sparkly studs in her ears but they weren't real diamonds. Justine-Tacky-Littlewood and Louise just had yucky bead friendship bracelets.

I so wanted everyone to envy me having a real gold heart locket worth a fortune. They'd all laugh at me if they knew it was a trashy old fairground prize. I couldn't let them find out.

'To me it's real gold, Peter,' I said firmly, threading it on a piece of string.

It didn't have exactly the right effect. I sidled into Adele's room while she was in the bathroom and had a quick rummage through her dressing-table drawers. I came across just the job, a white broderie anglaise blouse threaded with thin red velvet ribbon. I wondered about asking... but Adele was still a bit narked because I'd dressed up in her black high heels to

be a Spanish dancer and I'd stamped a little too vigorously and one of the silly heels fell off. She'd said I couldn't ever ever ever borrow her clothes again.

I didn't want to borrow her whole blouse, just the red velvet ribbon running round it, but I still had a funny feeling she'd object. So I had one quick tug at the ribbon and suddenly there it was, in my hand.

20

I charged back to my room and tied it with the gold heart. It looked great! Oh dear, if only it were *real* solid gold and worth something!

'It looks lovely on you, Tracy,' said Peter.

'Yes, it does,' I said, smoothing the ribbon and stroking the heart.

'So we're really sweethearts now?' Peter said eagerly.

'If you say so,' I said.

'Oh, I do! I really love you, Tracy.'

He waited, his head on one side.

'Do you love me, Tracy?'

'Oh, *Pete*. Look, I'm not into all that dopey lovey-dovey stuff.'

He blinked his big Bambi eyes, his lip starting to tremble.

'Don't look so *stricken*! It's not *you*, Peter. It's not personal at all. I'm never going to fall in love. I'm Tracy Beaker. I'm *immune*.'

Little did I know that sneaky baby Cupid was lurking in a corner, arrow poised, about to pierce my heart.

I did a little tap dance downstairs, my gold heart bouncing on the end

of the red ribbon. I paused at the window on the landing. You could see all the way down the drive to the gates at the end. I usually leant against this window and waited on Saturdays. I paused here today.

'Are you watching out for . . . anyone?' Peter asked delicately.

I nodded.

'I'll wait with you,' said Peter.

He didn't have anyone to watch for, not unless his own nan popped down a celestial ladder from heaven and shuffled up the drive in her Dr Scholl's. He was just keeping me company.

I was watching for my mum of course. She's going to come and see me very soon. I might just have mentioned this before. Justine-Relentlessly-Evil-Littlewood says my mum's forgotten all about me and isn't ever going to come and see me. But she is *sooo* wrong and if she says it again I'll punch her on the nose. Of course my mum's coming. Very very soon. On Saturday. That's what she said when I last saw her.

It was quite a long time ago but I remember every single second so very clearly. Mum took me out and we went for this incredibly posh meal. I couldn't *believe* the prices! It meant my mum thought the whole world of me. She let me order absolutely everything I fancied on the menu, with a double portion of French fries and then *two* puddings and *then* lots of little chocolates on a pretty saucer.

It was the best meal I'd ever had. I didn't hang on to it for very long. I was so excited to see my Mum that my tummy went fizz fizz fizz and I had to gallop in double-quick time to the ladies' where I was horribly sick. Mum was a bit cross with me then and I don't blame her because she'd forked out a small fortune on that meal then I'd wasted it all. But she mopped me up and we went to buy me a new top because the one I was wearing got a bit splashed. It wasn't just an ordinary T-shirt from Primark – it was *designer*. Mum didn't flinch as she flashed her credit card.

Then Mum took me to the cinema. I so hoped it was going to be one of Mum's films and I'd see her acting at last, but it was a cartoon film. It had a fairy-tale princess in it, with long golden hair just like my mum though. And then Mum took me back

to the Dumping Ground and I had a very severe attack of hayfever.

Mum told me I mustn't make such a silly fuss, she'd come and get me for good as soon as she could get everything sorted, and meanwhile she'd visit me as often as possible.

'Next Saturday?' I said, and Mum said, 'Sure.' She even called, 'See you Saturday' as she waved and went down the drive.

So I waited. I thought she meant the actual *next* Saturday but she didn't come. Then I realized she meant *a* Saturday. So I wait for her every Saturday, watching from the window to get the first glimpse of her. I stand at the window and stare out, concentrating hard. I stare at the gates and will Mum to walk through them.

So I stared and stared and stared, and Peter stood beside me, staring too. Then I heard Adele shouting that *someone* had been in her room messing about with her clothes, and I felt a little too prominent in my window-watching position. I scooted downstairs, Peter at my side, and went into our sitting room. Maxy was watching television while still eating his breakfast toast. He was so absorbed watching some silly cartoon that he frequently missed his mouth, smearing butter all over his cheeks and chin.

'Tracy's my Valentine sweetheart,' Peter said.

Maxy grunted, unimpressed.

'I think you should be Justine's sweetheart, Maxy. The minute she comes downstairs run and give her a great big kiss. Rub your face all over her,' I said.

'Really?' Maxy said indistinctly.

'Absolutely,' I said, although Peter frowned at me.

'*Swap Shop's* starting on the other channel,' said Peter. 'Let's watch that instead. It's good, isn't it, Tracy?'

I shrugged. I didn't know any of the Saturday morning shows because of my weekly vigil on the stairs, but I'd heard some of the other kids talking about it. There was this funny furry little fox telling silly jokes, and there was some young guy presenter, Billy or Barry or . . . 'Hi, I'm Barney.'

He was smiling straight out of the television – straight at *me*. His warm brown eyes shone and his cheeky face lit up. I loved his funny monkey T-shirt. He looked like a big  brother who loved fooling around and making jokes – and yet he had big strong arms that could give you a hug, just like a dad.

There was a *twang* in the room as that pesky little Cupid shot his arrow, and a *thunk* as it

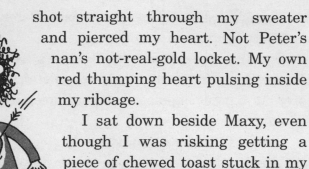

shot straight through my sweater and pierced my heart. Not Peter's nan's not-real-gold locket. My own red thumping heart pulsing inside my ribcage.

I sat down beside Maxy, even though I was risking getting a piece of chewed toast stuck in my ear. Peter sat neatly cross-legged on the other side of me.

'This is a good programme, Tracy,' he said. 'I love Basil Brush. And I like Barney too. Do you like him?'

'Yeah, he's OK,' I mumbled. Like! He was *fantastic*!

Barney smiled as if he could hear us.

'Who likes a hearty breakfast?' he asked, grinning, 'Cupid!'

I snorted with laughter.

'Did you get any Valentine cards today?' asked Barney. 'I didn't, sob sob.'

'I got hundreds!' said Basil Brush. 'I know a lot of foxy ladies – boom boom!'

Barney sighed and rolled his brown eyes. 'Here's a little Valentine verse just for you.'

He was looking straight at me!
'Roses are red,
Violets are blue,
Watch *Swap Shop* on Saturday
And I'll love you true.'
'I'll love *you*, Barney,' I said inside my head.

He nodded and gave me a wink. But our thrilling telepathy was suddenly obliterated by Justine-Foghorn-Littlewood barging into the room, shrieking with laughter over something stupid. Maxy hurled himself at her and nuzzled her neck romantically. He spread slime, snot and soggy toast all over her head, hair and sweater in a highly satisfactory fashion. She shrieked even louder.

Mike came running, convinced she was being murdered (I *wish*!). When he'd calmed her down he stayed to watch *Swap Shop* with us.

'I used to watch *Swap Shop* when *I* was a kid,' he said. 'And is that Basil Brush? He doesn't look quite the same. I'm sure his snout used to be more pointy. He looks a bit too cuddly now. Who's the scruffy guy with him? He used to be with Mr Derek.'

'Oh Mike, you are hopeless! That's Barney. Justine and I think he's seriously cool,' said Louise.

How dare they! He was *my* Barney!

27

'Yeah, we like his funky little bit of face-fuzz,' said Justine-Leery-Eyes-Littlewood, mopping herself with a J-cloth. 'Hey look, that girl wants to swap a karaoke kit for something else. Is she *mad*? I'd give anything for one. I'm going to phone in and offer to swap it for . . . What can I offer, Lou?'

'I could offer my hair-straightening kit now I've decided to go for the naturally curly look,' she said.

'I could swap my rubber Dumbo for it,' said Maxy.

'*You're* the Dumbo, Maxy! It's worth about five pence maximum after you've slobbered all over it,' said Justine-Spurn-Her-Sweetheart-Littlewood. 'You've got to swap something of equivalent value. A karaoke kit is worth *heaps*.'

'Do you want a karaoke kit, Tracy?' Peter said.

Of *course* I did. It would be so cool to plug it in and belt out a little number with proper musical accompaniment. Maybe I could even croon a ballad for Barney! Only what could I swap? My possessions were as manky as Maxy's. All my books were wrinkly because I read them in the bath. My skateboard buckled that time I played dodgem dustbins. My CD player broke when I dropped it down the stairs. I'd lost my left flashing trainer and my right footie boot and *both* my rollerblades. I didn't have anything – and yet I *so* wanted a karaoke machine.

I was sure I could sing better than the stars. It would be my chance to be discovered. Forget Amy, forget Lily. You're toast, Rhianna and Duffy. Tracy Beaker, singing superstar, is taking to the stage.

My heart started thumping. I fingered my gold heart locket. It wasn't real gold but it looked like it. Jenny and Mike and all the other kids except Peter thought it was real gold and worth a fortune. Worth way more than a karaoke machine. But I couldn't swap Peter's heart . . . could I?

It wasn't Peter's any more though. He'd given it to me. I could legitimately do what I liked with it: keep it in my treasure box, wear it on a ribbon, sell it to a jeweller, *swap it* . . . And it wasn't as if it was *worth* anything.

Justine-Out-To-Outdo-Me-Littlewood was already begging Mike to lend her his mobile.

'Quick, quick, I need to get through to *Swap Shop now*, Mike. Louise and I are offering to swap her hair-straightening kit.'

'Are you OK with this, Louise?' said Mike. 'It's *your* hair-straightening do-da.'

'Yes, that's fine. Justine and I will share the karaoke machine,' said Louise.

'That's what best friends are for. Sharing!' said Justine-Snatch-*My*-Friend-Littlewood.

I felt as if she'd punched me in the chest. My heart thumped. I suddenly put my arm round Peter.

'*We're* best friends, aren't we, Pete?' I said.

'Oh *yes*, Tracy,' said Peter, his big eyes shining. 'Sweethearts *and* best friends.'

'We'd like to share a karaoke kit, wouldn't we?' I said.

Peter nodded a little less certainly.

'If only we had something brilliant to swap,' I said. 'Something worth much much more than a silly old hair-straightening kit. Can you think of anything, Peter?'

Peter blinked, looking bewildered.

'Quick, quick, Justine's phoning already. We *have* to outbid her!' I said urgently. 'Think, Pete, think! Have we got *anything*?'

I fingered the heart locket ostentatiously (meaning I practically thrust it in Peter's face). He gazed at it, a little cross-eyed.

'Well . . . all I can think of is my nan's heart locket,' he said.

'Yes! Yes, of course! Oh well done, Peter! You're sure you don't mind?' I gabbled, pulling him over towards Mike.

'Well, it's your heart locket now, Tracy. Don't *you* mind?' said Peter.

'Of course I mind. Very much,' I said. 'But we both know it isn't really worth anything. And it looks pretty but it doesn't really *do* anything, does it? Not like a karaoke machine. I'll let you have first go if we can swap it.'

'Hey, Tracy, what are you talking about?' said Mike. 'What are you saying to Peter? You're not saying you want to swap his nan's *heart*?'

'It's OK, it's not *real* gold, so it's not like it's really valuable – only *they're* not to know,' I hissed, and I grabbed the phone from Justine-Long-Winded-Littlewood.

'Give that back, I haven't finished!' she shrieked.

'You've *had* your turn. It's *mine* now,' I insisted. 'Isn't that right, Pete?'

'Hey hey hey!' said the guy at the end of the phone. 'Stop squabbling, you lot!'

'Is that *you*, Barney?' I said, hanging onto the phone, fingers superglued to the handset.

'No, sorry, I'm not Barney. Or Basil Brush either.'

'Boom boom!' I said.

'Exactly,' said the person. 'I'm Ben. I just work for the programme. Now, are you all one family? I've got Justine's name down – and Louise too. Are they your sisters?'

'NO WAY!' I said. 'Take no notice of their pathetic offering. Whoever wants a boring old hair-straightening kit?'

'You certainly *need* one, Tracy Beaker. You look like your head's been plugged into a light socket,' yelled Justice-Big-Gob-Littlewood.

'Shut *up*, Justine,' I bellowed. 'This is my turn. Isn't it, Ben?' I said down the telephone.

'If you say so,' said Ben.

'I want to talk too!' said Maxy, grabbing for the phone with his revoltingly sticky paws.

'No, get *off*, Maxy! Yuck, you're getting slurp all over my skirt, stop it!'

'Are you watching *Swap Shop* with a whole bunch of friends?' said Ben.

'Do we *sound* like friends?' I asked, mega-exasperated. 'More like deadly enemies! We live in this Dumping Ground.'

'Tracy!' said Mike. 'Children's Home, *if* you please. And hurry up, that's my own personal phone and you're costing me a fortune.'

'I'm *trying* to hurry up,' I said. 'Listen, Ben, I've got this amazing gold locket. I just *know* that karaoke girl will want to swap for it.'

'Are you sure it's *your* gold heart locket, Tracy?' asked Ben. 'It's not your mum's?'

'Of course it's not my *mum's*. As if I'd want to swap it then!' I said. 'No, it's a long story. My friend Peter gave it to me, for Valentine's day, actually, but we both think a karaoke set would be *way* more exciting, don't we, Peter?'

I prodded him and he nodded, though his bottom lip was quivering for some reason.

'Well, if there's an interesting story attached to this heart maybe you and some of your friends – or deadly enemies – might like to come along to the *Swap Shop* studio next week. You could show off your gold locket, Tracy.'

'And I'll meet Barney?'

'You'll meet everyone – Melvyn, Basil Brush, Frosty the Snowman, Keith the swapping hamster – *and* Barney. I think it would be a great idea for all you guys to be in our skip full of kids. You and Peter and Justine and Louise and Maxy and any other of your pals in the Children's Home. You could try to swap a karaoke set for all of you. Tracy, you've gone very quiet. You're still there, aren't you?'

'Yes,' I said. 'Um, can you just run that past me again, Ben? You're saying I'm invited to the studio to meet Barney, and I'm going to be, like, on *television*? Me, Tracy Beaker?'

'*What*?' shrieked Justine-Totally-Jealous-Littlewood. 'Tracy Beaker's going to be on *Swap Shop*? That's not FAIR! It was all *my* idea. I phoned up first. *I* should be picked to go on television!'

'Pipe down you lot!' Mike bellowed. 'Would you mind handing me my phone, please? If *any* of you are appearing on television then *I* need to be involved. Shh, the lot of you!'

He talked long and earnestly, sometimes nodding, sometimes shaking his head, while we listened, holding our breath.

'Well, thank you so much. I'll e-mail you all the details,' said Mike, and he switched off his phone.

We all started clamouring. He held up his arms for silence.

'OK kids, they want six of you there at the studios next week for the show. It's all fixed.'

'HURRAY! HURRAY! HURRAY!' we shrieked, jumping up and down.

Justine-Still-Not-My-Friend-Littlewood hugged Louise. I was so jubilant I hugged Maxy, rendering myself seriously sticky, in need of a thorough hosing down. I went to hug Peter too but he hung back, rubbing his cuddle hankie against his nose.

'What's up, Peter? Come on, be *happy*, we're going to be on television!' I said, giving him a little shake.

'I'm not sure I *want* to be on television,' he said in a tiny voice, muffled behind his hankie.

'Of course you do. Don't worry, you don't have to *say* anything. I'll say it all for you.'

'Yeah, Tracy-Big-Blabbermouth,' said Justine-She-Can-Talk-Littlewood.

'You can just shut up, Justine. I don't know why *you're* jumping up and down like a jackass because *you're* not going. Or you, Louise. *I'm* the one they invited. Me, Tracy Beaker. *I* get to choose my five companions. Get it?'

'Stop shouting, Tracy,' said Jenny, coming in from the kitchen with a baby on either hip. 'What were you all yelling about? What's going on, Mike?'

'The kids are going to be on *Swap Shop* on the telly next week,' said Mike, grinning.

'Oh no they're not,' said Jenny.

'Oh yes we *are*,' I said, sounding like we were doing a pantomime routine.

'No, Tracy. I'm sorry, you *can't* be on television. There are all sorts of regulations about looked-after children. We'd never get permission in time,' said Jenny.

'Look, my mum's quite probably coming to see me this very Saturday so we can get her permission today,' I said.

'Now, Tracy, I know you'd love to see your mum, but you know she isn't really coming,' Jenny said very quietly.

'Yes, she is so!'

'Tracy, we're not even very sure where she *is* at the moment,' said Jenny.

'She's in Hollywood, I keep *telling* you! Are you deaf or stupid?' I yelled, hating Jenny.

'Ha ha ha, Tracy Beaker. *You* can't go but *I* can, because I see my dad heaps and he'd be over the moon to watch me on television,' crowed Justine-Impossibly-Hateful-Littlewood.

'No, you're not any of you going. It's against the rules and would involve endless paperwork,' said Jenny.

'Look, I've said they can go and they're *going*,' said Mike. 'Any other kid in the country can go on telly so why can't they? I don't care if it gets us into trouble. I'm taking them and that's that.'

We all fell on Mike, giving him huge hugs.

But it was Jenny who battled with all the phone calls and paperwork. I passed by her office and saw her simultaneously typing an e-mail, talking on the phone and jiggling a whimpering baby on her lap.

37

The baby kept trying to hurl herself onto her head just to add to Jenny's problems.

'That baby thinks she's a lemming,' I said. 'Here, I'll take her, shall I?'

I scooped the baby up. She blinked at me in surprise and then reached eagerly for the gold heart round my neck.

'Naughty! I don't want your tiny teeth-marks all over it. It's my special swap for Saturday,' I said.

Jenny snorted and muttered a very rude word about *Swap Shop*.

'Um! I wouldn't half get told off if *I* said that. Jenny, I *can* go on *Swap Shop* can't I? I can't miss this huge big chance to star on television. I might get discovered, impress them so much they offer me my own kid's show. After all, acting's in my blood! Look at my mum, the famous Hollywood movie star.'

'Oh, Tracy,' said Jenny.

'She *is*,' I said. 'Just you wait, she'll be coming for me any day now.'

Jenny nodded wearily.

I waited, joggling the baby.

'Jenny . . .'

'Yes, Tracy.'

'You said you don't know where my mum is.'

'Mm.' Jenny reached out and stroked my arm. 'We've been trying to get in touch. Apparently she's moved on from her last known address.'

'Because she's in Hollywood. *Obviously*,' I said.

We looked at each other.

'Right,' said Jenny, sighing.

'Hey, hey, I told you no biting!' I said to the baby, who was drooling all over the heart.

'Tracy, about Peter's nan's locket—'

'It's *my* locket now.'

'Yes I know. But I don't think you realize that it's maybe very upsetting for Peter that you want to swap it straight away.'

'But it's not real gold. It's not worth anything, Jenny, I promise.'

'What about sentimental value?'

'You're talking to me, Tracy Beaker. I'm not into sentiment, Jenny,' I said briskly.

I did pursue the matter a little further with Peter though. I cornered him that night when we both had occasion to go to the linen cupboard for clean sheets.

'You're sure you're OK about me swapping my heart locket, Peter?' I said.

'Yes, that's fine, Tracy,' he said, snuffling into his nanny hankie.

'It'll be *sooo* great to have a karaoke machine, won't it?' I said. 'We'll sing a duet, you and me, Peter. That will be fun, won't it?'

'Yes, Tracy,' Peter mumbled.

I gently unhooked his hankie from his nose and prodded the corners of his mouth. 'Smile, then!'

He smiled obediently. So that was all right then.

He wasn't smiling early on Saturday morning. He was crying.

'Oh, for goodness' sake, Pete, what's *up* with you? This is our big day,' I said, giving him a little shake.

'I've-lost-my-hankie!' he sobbed.

'What? Oh, give me a break! Get a tissue from the bathroom.'

'No, it's my nan's hankie, it got mixed up in the sheets and they're all higgledy-piggledy in the laundry basket and I can't *find* it!' Peter wailed.

'I'm not sure I'd *want* to find it in amongst a load of damp smelly sheets!' I said. 'Oh, cheer up, Peter. I'm sure Jenny will find it for you, and if she doesn't she'll get you a brand new hankie.'

'I don't want a new hankie, I want my *old* hankie that belonged to my nan,' Peter wept.

'Now look! This is our big day. It means *sooo* much to me. I'm going to meet Barney and get a karaoke machine! So don't spoil it for me, OK?' I said.

Peter blinked at me, sniffling. 'I'm sorry, Tracy,' he squeaked. He tried to smile again, even though the tears were still streaming down his cheeks.

'You are such a *baby*, Peter,' said Justine-Utterly-Lacking-Compassion-Littlewood. 'Hey, Lou, do you think I look OK in this top or should I change it?'

'It's lovely, keep it on. But what about me?' said Louise. 'I'm not sure about wearing pink. Is it, like, *too* girly?'

'Excuse me!' I said. 'As if it matters. No one will be looking at you. *I'm* the one doing the swap. You'll just be in the background, *lurking*.'

'Pulling faces behind you,' said Justine-Can't-Ever-Be-Trusted-Littlewood.

'I can pull really scary faces, look,' said Maxy, pulling his eyelids down and his nose up, grinning like a gargoyle.

'You're seriously scary all the time, Maxy,' said Mike, pretending to cower away from him. 'Right, you guys, are we ready for the off? One, two, three, four, five . . . Where's Adele? Adele, come on!'

'I'll get her,' I said, charging up the stairs.

41

Melvyn

I was worried she'd changed her mind. She'd said she didn't want to go on a silly little kids' programme, thank you very much – but she gave into my pleading when she caught a glimpse of Barney's pal Melvyn on the television.

'He looks kind of cute,' she'd said. 'I love the way he does his hair. OK, Tracy, if it means all that much to you I'll come. *If* I feel like it on the day.'

'Adele, Adele, *please* feel like coming! You're my best friend. You jolly well have to support me,' I said now, barging into her room.

'Hey, hey, I'm just putting on my make-up,' said Adele.

She looked incredible: amazing outlined eyes, pearly lips, glitter on her cheeks, just like a fashion model.

'Oh, wow, you look wonderful. Can *I* have some make-up too, Adele? Please please please make me up to look like you,' I begged, although I was conscious of Mike downstairs bellowing at us to get a move on.

'You're not old enough for proper make-up, Tracy,' said Adele.

'Just a speck of lippy,' I pleaded.

'You're lippy enough already,' said Adele. 'How about a splodge of red lipstick on your nose – the comic clown effect? It'll match your red velvet ribbon round your neck!' She scribbled scarlet on my nose. I shrieked – but she took her tissue and wiped it straight *off*.

'Come on, then, Tracy. You look fine just as you are, I promise,' said Adele, ruffling my corkscrew curls. She was staring at my customized locket chain. 'Why does that ribbon look weirdly familiar?'

I shrugged and rushed her downstairs hurriedly. Jenny and all the littlies waved us goodbye and wished us luck. We all climbed into the mini van and we were off.

There was a five minute squabble about who was sitting where, everyone trying to steer well clear of Maxy, though Jenny had attacked him with an entire packet of wet wipes. Mike distracted us with a sing-song, and most of us joined in, practising for when I had my karaoke kit. Peter didn't sing very loudly. His voice was just a little mouse squeak.

As we got nearer and nearer the studio I found my tummy went tight and all *I* could manage was a squeak. My heart was going thump thump thump. I was about to meet Barney and be on television and it was so exciting – but oh-so-scary too. What if Barney didn't take any notice of me? What if I couldn't think of anything to say? I leaned forward and mumbled something of the sort into Mike's ear.

'You can't *help* noticing you, Tracy. And I've never *ever* known you at a loss for words,' he said.

We arrived at the studio and Mike announced to the doorman that we were Tracy Beaker and Party.

I loved that.

'I'm Tracy Beaker and you are my party!' I sang.

'You're Tracy Beaker and you are so *farty*,' sang Justine-Very-Vulgar-Littlewood.

We all had to get signed in, me and my party, and then we were led to a *dressing room*. I wanted it to have TRACY BEAKER, SUPERSTAR! on the door, but it just had a plain old number. Still, it was a very swish room, with a big mirror and two stylish sofas.

'Of course, this is pretty bog-standard compared with my *mum's* dressing rooms,' I said. 'She has white velvet sofas. They give her a new spotless one each week. And there's a chandelier and a white rug so soft she sinks in it up to her ankles.'

No one seemed to be listening to me, not even Peter. He was sucking his thumb, his chin on his chest.

'For goodness sake, Pete, you'll fuse all the cameras if you go into the studios with a face like that,' I said. I gave him a little prod. I wanted him to prod me back. He didn't. He just bent over further, his knees buckling.

'Come here, little pal,' said Mike, putting his arm round him. 'Don't worry about the hankie, I'm sure Jenny will find it for you. Or we'll get you another special hankie.'

'There isn't another one. Not one that belonged to my

nan,' Peter mumbled around his thumb. 'It's all I've got left of her.'

Mike leaned over Peter's head, looking at me.

'Do you hear what he's saying, Tracy?' he said.

I didn't *want* to hear. My heart was still going thump thump thump. Then there was a knock on my dressing room door and there was *Barney*!

'It's really *you*, Barney!' I gasped.

'No, actually I'm a cardboard cut-out,' he said, laughing. 'Hi, you must be Tracy.'

He picked me out! He knew me as soon as our eyes met!

'How did you know I'm Tracy?' I asked, thrilled.

'Oh, you're just how I imagined. And maybe your heart locket gave me a little bit of a clue. Oh dear though, Tracy, it looks a very special gold locket. I'm not sure we can let you swap it if it's really valuable.'

'No, it's fine, Barney. It's not solid gold,' I said hastily. 'It isn't really worth much, is it, Peter?'

Peter shook his head, his thumb still stoppering his mouth.

'And we're desperate to get that karaoke kit, aren't we, Peter?' I said.

Peter nodded this time, still mute.

'Well, we'll do our best to get it for you, kids,' said Barney. 'I think we're ready for you in the studio now. Come and meet Melvyn and Basil.'

We trooped along behind him. I hopped and skipped until I was beside him, staring up at him smiling and smiling and smiling.

'Are you excited about being on television, Tracy?' said Barney.

'You bet I am,' I said. I tried fluttering my eyelashes at him.

'Have you got something in your eyes, sweetheart?' said Barney. 'Try blinking hard.'

It was blinking hard trying to concentrate. I couldn't take my eyes off Barney and his soft hair and his big brown eyes and the little fuzzy down on his upper lip. My heart ached where the arrow had struck.

We trooped into the studio and stepped over snaky cables to the brightly coloured set. There were guys dressed up as lions and tigers and bears, a big Frosty the Snowman, children milling around, and a huge tank full of lime green gunge.

'A swimming pool!' Maxy yelled, hurtling towards it.

Mike managed to rugby-tackle him just as he was about to dive straight in.

'He's a game little chap,' said Barney, chuckling. 'But what's up with you, little guy?' He bent down to talk to Peter. 'Why are you all droopy-poopy? Don't you want to be on television?'

'*Tracy* wants to be on television,' Peter mumbled.

'And do you do what Tracy says, eh?' said Barney. 'Is she the boss?'

'She's not *my* boss,' said Justine-Can't-Bear-To-Be-Ignored-Littlewood.

'Tracy *is* a bit bossy,' said Peter. 'But I don't mind. She's my sweetheart.'

'Aah!' said Barney.

'I'm his sweetheart but he's not *mine*,' I whispered into Barney's ear.

Barney nodded though he didn't look as if he absolutely understood. But there was no time to elaborate as we were being prodded into position for the start of the show. I had to sit on a special chair beside Barney and Basil Brush popped up beside him.

'Oooh! It's a little doggy!' yelled Maxy.

'I am not a *dog*, little boy,' said Basil Brush, giving him a poke with his pointy snout. 'Why did the dog kennel leak, humm? It needed a new *woof*! Boom Boom!'

'Silly doggy,' said Maxy, unimpressed.

'Quit being a pain, Maxy,' said Justine-Interfering-Littlewood.

She stood right behind my chair, and when

I peered round at her she was pouting at the camera in sick-making fashion. Louise was simpering too and Adele was striking a pose, hand on her hip.

Peter was standing a little apart. He reached for the bottom of his sweater and held it awkwardly up to his nose, rubbing against it. He was so hopelessly lost without his nan's hankie. It was all he had left of her. Apart from the heart locket . . .

My own heart went thump thump thump.

'We're on air in ten seconds,' said Barney. 'Good luck, kids.'

My heart was thumping so hard I thought it would burst right out my sweater. The *Swap Shop* music started and Barney and Basil chatted away, welcoming everyone to the show.

'We're particularly delighted to welcome Tracy here, with all her friends—'

'And enemies,' muttered Justine-Can't-Shut-Up-Littlewood.

'—who live in a Children's Home and very much want a karaoke machine to have fun with,' said Barney. 'So what have you got to swap, Tracy?'

'I've got this very special unique gold locket,' I said, holding it up.

'And who gave it to you?' said Barney.

'My friend Peter gave it to me on Valentine's Day,' I said.

Justine and Louise made yuck noises behind my back. Peter put his hand up, trying valiantly to smile.

'So you two are little lovebirds, eh?' said Barney.

'What do you call two birds in love?' asked Basil Brush. 'Soppy! Boom boom!'

'I think they're very sweet,' said Barney. 'So who gave *you* this lovely locket, Peter?'

'It was my nan's,' Peter whispered. Two tears spilled down his cheeks.

'Oh, Peter, *don't* cry,' I said.

'I'm not crying, Tracy. I – I've just got hayfever,' Peter snuffled.

I looked at him. My heart gave such a thump I had to clutch my chest. What was the matter with me? Why were there tears in my own eyes? I was Tracy Beaker, tough as old boots. Why was I worrying so? The silly old locket wasn't worth anything.

I couldn't kid myself any more. The locket was worth the whole world to Peter – and he'd given it to me.

'I can't *do* this!' I wailed. 'I'm sorry, Barney. Please don't get mad at me. I know I'm wrecking your programme and I so want a karaoke machine but I *can't* swap the heart. It's all Peter's got left of his nan now. It's maybe not actually *real* gold but that doesn't matter, it's worth much more because it was so special to him and yet he gave it to me. So now I'm going to give it back to him. Here you are, Pete.' I took it off and handed it to him.

'Oh, Tracy! We wanted the karaoke machine!' said Justine-No-Heart-At-All-Littlewood.

'Well, maybe we can see if you can *win* a karaoke machine,' said Barney. 'We've got our three teams set up to brave the dreaded Gungulator. How about you guys challenging the winners? Just two of you. Let's see – Tracy and Justine!'

'But we can't be in a team *together*! We're deadly enemies.' I protested.

'There's no way I'm ever being part of a team with *Tracy*,' said Justine. 'I'll be in a team with Louise.'

'No, no, Peter and me will be a team!' I insisted.

'Count *me* out of any team. I'm not going in that green gunge!' said Adele in horror.

'I'll go, I'll go, I *love* green gunge,' Maxy shouted.

'Hey, hey, shh you lot. Do you want to give it a go or not?' said Barney. He grinned at me. He grinned at Justine. 'Go on, girls. Swallow your differences.'

I didn't want to let Barney down. I looked at Justine. She looked at me. We both swallowed. Then we nodded.

So we sat and watched the rest of the show. Peter nestled right up to me, the heart locket round his neck.

'You can have it back though, Tracy. It *is* yours,' he whispered.

'We'll share it, Pete, OK. Now be quiet, I need to watch this game to see how it works.'

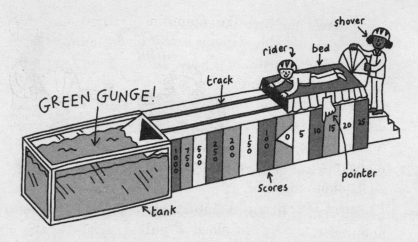

GREEN GUNGE!

track

rider

bed

shover

tank

Scores

pointer

One kid got in a bed on a trolley. The other kid shoved the bed. They scored points the further it went. But if the shove was too hard then the bed went right off the scale and the kid tipped straight into the green slime.

We watched, we waited, we wondered . . . The Zebras team were defeated first. Then the Bees. So we had to beat the Tigers – with a final score of 100.

'We'll beat that easy-peasy,' I said to Justine.

'Of course we will,' she said.

'Good luck, Tracy!' said Peter.

'Good luck, Justine!' said Louise.

'Good luck both of you,' said Barney. 'Right, Tracy, you get on the bed first.' I got on the bed and Justine stood behind me.

'Watch what you're doing now, Justine. Don't be too feeble. Give a really firm push – but not *too* hard!'

'Oh, quit bossing me, Tracy Beaker,' Justine snapped and gave my bed a shove.

I shot forward.

I passed 50, then 100, 150 . . . I was slowing now, and I so needed to slow! I pulled hard on the end of the bed, trying to brake, but it was no use. I was edging further and further forward, past 200, past 250, past 500, oh no, past 750 and then . . .

SPLASH!

I screamed and swallowed a bucketful of icy-cold lime-green slime. I struggled to my feet, shaking my head, while the

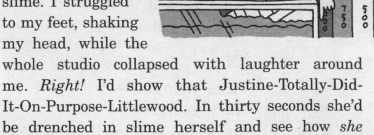

whole studio collapsed with laughter around me. *Right!* I'd show that Justine-Totally-Did-It-On-Purpose-Littlewood. In thirty seconds she'd be drenched in slime herself and see how *she* liked it.

I heaved myself out of the pool, snorting slime. Justine was practically wetting herself.

'Oh, help, it's a green slime sludge monster! No, wait a minute, it's Tracy Beaker!'

'You wait!'I said, as she clambered onto the bed and I took charge of the controls.

'Remember, Tracy, you want that karaoke set,' Barney called quickly. 'If Justine goes in the slime you'll lose your chance of winning one!'

My heart went . . . you've got it, thump thump thump! I sooo wanted to dump Justine in the green gunge the way she'd dumped me. But if I did then we'd lose our karaoke set and I sooo wanted that too. Not just for me. Peter and I could sing our duets . . .

I looked at Peter.

'Go for it, Tracy!' he yelled.

'Yeah, crack it, girl!' Adele shouted.

'Yes yes yes!' Maxy burbled.

'You can do it, Tracy,' said Mike.

'Do it for everyone, Tracy,' said Barney, giving me the thumbs-up sign.

I took a deep breath and gave Justine a sharp edgy shove that set her rolling. She went past 50, 100, 150, 200 ... She was yelling like crazy now, ducking her head – but then she slowed to a dramatic halt, spot on the 250 sign. We'd beaten the others! Yay, we'd won!!!

'Well done, Tracy! You've won your karaoke machine for you and all your mates. I knew you could do it!' Barney shouted happily.

'I knew I could too!' I said. My heart went thumpety-thumpety-thump

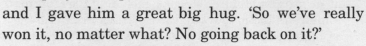

and I gave him a great big hug. 'So we've really won it, no matter what? No going back on it?'

'Yes, really,' said Barney.

'Great!' I said – and before Justine-Ever-Deadly-Enemy-Littlewood could get out of the bed I gave it one more shove. She shot straight into the green gunge. That wiped the grin off her face!

Jacqueline Wilson is one of Britain's most outstanding writers for young readers. She is the most borrowed author from British libraries and has sold over 25 million books in this country. As a child, she always wanted to be a writer and wrote her first 'novel' when she was nine, filling countless exercise books as she grew up. She started work at a publishing company and then went on to work as a journalist on *Jackie* magazine (which was named after her) before turning to writing fiction full-time.

Jacqueline has been honoured with many of the UK's top awards for children's books, including the Guardian Children's Fiction Award, the Smarties Prize and the Children's Book of the Year. She was the Children's Laureate for 2005-2007, was awarded an OBE in 2002 and made a Dame in 2008.

'A brilliant writer of wit and subtlety whose stories are never patronising and are often complex and many-layered' *The Times*

'It's the combination of accessible stories and humorous but penetrating treatment of big emotional themes that makes this writer so good' *Financial Times*

Join the FREE Jacqueline Wilson Fan Club at
www.jacquelinewilson.co.uk